People Will Always Ask

T.Remington

Published by Anomalous Works NYC, 2024.

PEOPLE WILL ALWAYS ASK

First edition. November 23, 2024.

Copyright © 2024 T.Remington.

ISBN: 979-8230844044

Written by T.Remington.

Also by T.Remington

Plague Year New York City 2020
Nice Try Short Stories
People Will Always Ask

For Robert

Fixing a Broken Elephant

A broken church is one thing but a broken elephant is quite another. You don't see anyone climbing ladders and fitting the elephant with a new trunk, do you? But the moment the bombing ended, they went at it like busy little ants throwing up ladders and scaffolding, hammering throughout the night. Why is a church more important than an elephant?

That's not a rhetorical question. I demand an answer. That's ok. I'll wait.

I thought as much. You don't know either. No one does. I've asked everyone.

I'll tell you something. I knew that elephant when it was whole. Yes, yes I did. I know that elephant's name. No, I'm not going to tell you. What difference does it make now? It's a broken, unrepairable elephant. The elephant is out and the church is in, although only God knows why. Some people have very odd priorities, I've found. I wish they'd take a break or something over there. Must they pound and clatter and saw all day and night?

Say, you look familiar. Where have I seen your face before? Wait. Don't tell me. It was in the newspaper. Recently. Wait, I know. You're the one in charge of all the hubbub over there, aren't you? You're the Chief Architect in Charge of Restoration of that holy pile of rubble. Well, well, well.

Interesting that they put a foreigner in charge. No offense but people around here are distrustful and for good reason. I realize that you're not one of the ones that was dropping bombs around here and all. That would be rich, though, wouldn't it? First, you bomb us and then come in and rebuild. Say, that's actually kind of brilliant. No, no. I understand. You're not one of them. Your country was neutral you say? Well, I've got an opinion about that, but I'll keep it to myself.

Say, if you're as good as the newspaper was saying and all, I have a proposition for you. No money in it, but since you're part of this great humanitarian effort that's working to get our country back on its feet, this would go a long way towards bringing people around.

See that elephant over there? What do you think?

People will always ask if that's his real name but no one's ever gotten a straight answer out of Twitch. By "people" I mean tourists and, yes, even a town as forgettable as San Sierlo gets tourists in this part of the country. Baby, this is Tuscany and there's not a square kilometer that doesn't boast at last fifteen tourists and that's in the off season.

Danny and I moved here in 2004 after that war criminal was reelected in the U.S. I'd already begun working with an Italian attorney to establish dual citizenship and the morning after the election we booked one-way flights. It was a lot trickier to settle in another country than we'd expected and we thought we were coming into this with open eyes. Language was just the beginning (Thanks a pantload for refusing to teach us Italian, Mom).

Considering we're a couple of city kids, I think we've done all right with our little grocery store/cafe here, though. Sure, Florence would have been ideal if we could have afforded that but now that I'm used to small-town life here it's pretty sweet. Mostly.

Twitch introduced himself to us the day we put the open for business sign out front for the first time. And when I say "introduced himself" what I mean is that a tiny, slightly stooped person of indeterminate gender stuck their head in the open doorway and crooned something wordless and even kind of tuneless but lovely nevertheless. Danny stopped stocking the shelves and I came out from the tiny kitchen, wiping my hands on my apron, something I'd never have been caught dead wearing back in Chicago.

Before we could figure anything out our already best friend, Dr. Scalfaro, came in and patted the little crooner on the shoulder.

"I see you've met our Twitch."

Dr. S. likes to speak English with us. No one else in the village speaks anything but the local dialect so the good doctor spends a fair amount of time — and money — sitting in our cafe talking. His habit of pontificating can be tedious but that's a small price to pay for having an in.

San Sierlo is almost a caricature of an insular old-world village. The butcher's parents moved here after the war when he was a toddler and he's still considered to be *non da qui,* not from here.

So having the respected Dr. Scalfaro take up with us is probably at least half of the reason for our success.

The other half, surprisingly enough, is Twitch.

According to Dr. S., Twitch's mother was a child herself. She was the youngest daughter of the local rum-runner, or whatever they're called here. It's the good doctor's considered medical opinion — mind you, Dr. S. is a retired dermatologist who practiced in Florence and retired here, his hometown— that Twitch's retardation (Dr. S's word, not mine) is due to the young age of his mother. I'd go out on a limb here and suggest that the poor kid was born with fetal alcohol syndrome. And that's my more benign conclusion.

There were several kids who looked sort of like Twitch in the special education classes I used to substitute teach back in Chicago. But they sure didn't sound like Twitch.

No one sounds like Twitch.

We didn't start out thinking of having a dinner hour here but thanks to Twitch we're stuck with it now. And, yes yes yes, we're making money hand over fist but running the store and the cafe from 7 am until 10 pm daily is grinding us down pretty badly.

It started out with Twitch simply coming by in the afternoon to sit in the shade and do that croony-hummy thing he does instead of talking. I began serving a late afternoon snack after the heat of the day and that morphed into adding a dinner menu. Now Danny's got the store, I cook constantly, he does the books, and Twitch is becoming fucking famous. I'm not even kidding when I tell you that the little prodigy got a write up in some digital nomad's blog and the floodgates opened for real.

We don't talk about things but the strain is there. Even Dr. S. seems to pick up on it and fills our silences with amusing anecdotes about the people passing by.

As I'm getting to where I understand the local dialect better, I hear things. I could probably hold my end in a conversation here now, but I continue to pretend to be the dumb American who stumbles over textbook Italian and that helps. The ladies at the post office were talking the other day about how good it is that the Americans have provided poor poor Twitch with a safe place to sit and do that stupid crooning. I smiled and haltingly asked for Mom's latest care package. Little do those old biddies realize. And how would they? No locals can ever get a table at our place which isn't exactly endearing us in the village.

"We can't keep going like this." Danny looks like hell.

"Look, I'll close up and clean everything. You go on to bed."

"So you can sleep in tomorrow."

"Right. So I can sleep in until 7 am when the deliveries start."

"7 am isn't 5 am." He pauses and then hits me with: "You know how long it's been since we've had sex?"

Oh, Christ. I knew this was coming. I smooth my face and hope that little eye roll went unnoticed. It didn't.

"You don't know because you like it this way, don't you?"

"Danny, go to bed. We'll talk about hiring someone tomorrow. I'll ask Dr. S. if he can recommend someone."

"That's right. Change the subject." Danny's just reaching for the wine — like he needs more to drink — when that soft crooning wafts in the open door. Twitch must have come back, the damned little savant darling.

We sit silently and stare at each other. Danny drops his hand. I cover it with mine.

"Fuck the mess. Let's go to bed, love." I smile at him and wait.

Florence isn't as nice as I thought it would be. I suppose there are worse jobs than delivering Amazon Prime packages although it really sucks when the weather's bad. Oh, look, another postcard from Danny.

Now that he's got his little empire humming along up there in San Sierlo with five – count 'em, five - employees, he writes almost every week. Good for him. He got the business in the divorce.

But I got Twitch.

"C'mon, buddy. Let's get to it."

Twitch is the best roommate. Never complains about anything and is happy to sit out next to me in the evenings and croon, attracting tourists and Fiorentini alike. I draw my weird little drawings and sell them but most of the money that goes into our terra cotta bucket is because of Twitch.

On our way back to our two rooms I always stop by Twitch's favorite shop and buy him something nice. I think he's happy. Who can tell? He never says a word.

I guess I knew Dr. Scalfaro would track us down eventually. Jesus, you would have thought I'd kidnapped Twitch, which, ok, yes I suppose I did. I mean, he came willingly enough and all, but yeah, ok. So I kidnapped a mute orphan who slept in the back of the church.

Everything starts out friendly enough with Dr. S. complimenting me on how cozy and nice our rooms are. He brought wine and I bring out the regulatory loaf of crusty bread. I know why he's here and he knows I know but there are niceties to be observed. So we observe them. Eventually, he gets around to the reason for his visit.

"I have come to bring our Twitch home."

"He's happy here!"

"How do you even know?" The first glint of something to be wary of appears in dear old Dr. Scalfaro's watery blue eyes.

"Look at him. Twitch, baby, you like it here, right?" Even as I'm saying this I know I'm full of it.

During my time in San Sierlo, Dr. S. was always a jolly sort who liked bad puns and tipped generously. I never would have guessed he could be so scary. It's taking every bit of my old Southside Chicago balls to stand up to him but I can't lose Twitch. Too bad. I'm going to lose Twitch. I can fight it but Dr. Scalfaro's right. This isn't the place for Twitch and we all know it.

The poor kid sits there and looks back and forth between the two of us as Dr. Scalfaro starts throwing Twitch's few things into a bag he brought. He closes the bag, fixes me with a poisonous glare, and holds out his hand to Twitch who simply stares at it.

"*Vieni, ragazzo mio. È il momento di andare.*" To Twitch and then to me, "It's time for him to come home. You shouldn't have done this."

But Twitch doesn't move. I dare to hope. It's not like he's a minor...I don't think.

Dr. S. lets loose with a stream of something in the local dialect directed at Twitch. He's trying for kind and persuasive but his temper gets the better of him. Twitch shrinks as the doctor's voice gets louder. Dr. S. sees this and tries to tone it down some. I wait.

Eventually, the old man runs out of steam.

I pick up the bag, reach for Twitch's hand, and put the bag into it. He looks so relieved I think I'll cry. Silently, I put Twitch's other tiny hand into Dr. Scalfaro's and sit down heavily on the side of the bed. I have no idea what I'm going to do now without Twitch. Go back to the United States? Good Christ, not that. And Danny and I thought things when *Bush* was in office had been a nightmare.

"Come with us. Come back to San Sierlo." Dr. S. is back to being the kind, elderly gentleman. Twitch starts crooning.

"Danny won't like that. It'll create trouble."

Dr. Scalfaro straightens slightly. "I have found your Danny to be a very sensible man. He won't be any trouble. After all, you're not. Are you?" He smiles.

"Ready Twitch?"

Now Twitch is smiling ear to ear and that familiar croon is sounding more like a jig.

Hümdinger's Cats or Don't Open That Crate!

When Fritz got the job at the Hümdinger Research Center he was thrilled. He and Maggie went out for a fancy dinner and everything. He thought he knew what working in an animal test lab would be like. He was wrong.

The rats. Working with them turned out to be easy once he got past that initial stomach-clutch when handling them. It turned out that caring for rats was super easy and preparing them for "sac" — shorthand for sacrificing which is the euphemism for killing — was basically just another workday chore. Even caring for the ones whose limbs had been broken or had other terrible things done to them wasn't such a big deal. They were rats.

The white New Zealand rabbits were tougher. It was very difficult to prepare them for saccing. They were so gentle and trusting. Fritz didn't sleep well for weeks after preparing fifteen of those sweet bunnies for sac. Maggie suggested he think about going back into therapy.

Fritz knew other labs experimented on sheep and even horses or goats or dogs or monkeys. Hümdinger mostly worked with rats and rabbits. Until the day eight crates of cats from Baltimore showed up.

Fritz was the one who usually arranged for new deliveries but Professor Schrödinger came out to sign off on the crates.

"My new experiment, Fritz, very exciting stuff." Professor Schrödinger handed the clipboard back to the delivery people and instructed Fritz to stack the crates in the far corner of her lab. "Leave them for tonight."

Fritz was surprised to find Professor Schrödinger already in the lab when he arrived the next morning. He was even more surprised at her mussed hair and wrinkled lab coat.

"Good morning, Professor."

She seemed a little dazed and began walking over towards the crates. When Fritz reached to begin uncrating the cats, cats who seemed oddly silent, she stopped him.

"Don't."

"I'm sorry, Professor. Would you like me to come back later?"

Fritz hesitated. He had twenty rats to get to Dr. Everett's lab and needed to get these cats uncrated first. Professor Schrödinger seemed to be ready to say something but paused and began walking from crate to crate, pressing her face against the wood briefly and listening intently.

Fritz waited. He liked Professor Schrödinger but hoped she'd get herself sorted out soon. Dr. Everett would be a real pain if he didn't get his rats on time.

"Well, what do you think? Are they alive or are they dead?" Professor Schrödinger asked Fritz.

Fritz just stood there, dumbfounded.

"Exactly!" Professor Schrödinger's face shone as she rushed to her computer and began typing quickly. Fritz shifted uncomfortably.

"You can arrange for them to be returned to the supplier. The experiment was a success."

Fritz found out from Dr. Everett's administrative assistant about Professor Schrödinger's admission to the state psychiatric facility. He also found out that due to supplier error those crates had been shipped empty.

He gave his notice that day.

Not One. Not Two. Not Not Two.

Sparky had begun meditating really to get away from Mummy and that part wasn't working out so well. Mummy would pop her head into the room to see if he wanted his tea yet or would vacuum the hallway, chirping a cheery greeting outside his closed door before moving on to do the stairs. When he'd go to the zendo to sit, she'd stop by with treats for everyone and so had become a big hit with the sensei who asked about her all the time.

Then Sparky found the perfect place.

He began "sitting" zazen in the trunk of the car, pulling the trunk almost shut and arranging himself comfortably. It was dark. It was quiet. And, somehow, this is where Mummy didn't ever come looking for him. It was here in the dark, in the musty silence, that his monkey mind could really get to jumping. Doing just as his sensei, Mister McKinley, had counseled, Sparky watched his thoughts without attaching importance to them.

One day he climbed out of the trunk and slid quietly back into the house to find Mummy sitting on the edge of the chintz loveseat in the corner, with her hands folded and her eyes downcast. He moved carefully past her and went to get his tea. Mummy? Sitting? Well, imagine that!

After that Mummy began coming along to the zendo to sit (still bringing treats, of course). They never talked about their sitting practice and Sparky continued using the trunk of the car to sit.

After Pop had left with Miss Samples, his secretary, Mummy had had some kind of breakdown, attaching herself tightly to Sparky. It was as if she couldn't stand being two; she needed to be one with someone. Sparky probably should have known better than to have moved back in with her at that point, but finding decent work was tough and he did feel badly for her. He thought he could move back in temporarily to save some money and, at the same time, show Mummy that being two was right and proper.

Now they weren't one, but they weren't two either. Sparky began waking at the same time as Mummy and, without a word, they'd have their tea and toast. Then Mummy would go into the front room and Sparky would go off to the garage to climb into the trunk of the car. After that, again without talking about it, they'd go out to do the shopping for the day, taking flowers and groceries to Aunt Priss and bringing the mail around to the twins who were up in years and didn't get out much.

Sparky found an odd and unexpected comfort in their routine. They'd go off to sit at the zendo at the end of the day and were usually in bed before ten each night. Once Mummy came into the bathroom as Sparky was brushing his teeth and he was startled to find that he could see through his face and see Mummy's.

This couldn't be good.

The next morning, he went off to the garage and got into the trunk just like every other day after seeing Mummy go into the front room. The sensei had assigned them koans recently and Sparky settled into the frothy jumpy bit that always preceded calming down to contemplate his koan. He had this idea that stretching out would help. Even laying down, his mind seemed especially active this morning, so it took a while before he was aware that the car was moving.

Startled, he pushed against the trunk and found it was tightly closed. He could hear traffic outside and tried not to panic. He really should have told Mummy about his sitting place. Well, she couldn't be going far, so all he had to do was relax and they'd get to where they were going soon enough. Then he could pound on the trunk. He tried to go back to his koan, but the swaying and turning and starting and stopping of the car were too disorienting. He felt nauseous and the panic began to rise again. The car picked up speed. Sparky couldn't help himself and began pounding on the trunk, shoving his feet hard against the back of the backseat. Mummy turned on the radio and drove faster. (It was....Mummy, right?)

He began yelling and kicking harder. He'd seen in TV shows that you could kick in the back seat of the car from the trunk. Mummy took a turn hard, not slowing down much at all and Sparky was tumbled away from his kicking and hit his head against the jack stand. He was dazed now and couldn't remember which way to kick. Mummy turned up the radio and the Beatles loudly yeah yeah yeahed, almost covering the screeching of metal against metal.

Sparky was sobbing now, his throat felt raw from screaming. This was it. He knew it; now he'd really be one and only one for all eternity. Then the car stopped. Not dramatically with squealing brakes; just a nice quiet stop. The radio was snapped off and Sparky heard the driver's side door open and close. Would he hug his Mummy or attack her when she opened the trunk?

But he heard her walking away from the car; then there were voices that moved further away. He began to wildly kick and pound against the trunk, croaking in terror. Wait! Come back! Don't leave me here! The voices stopped, but nothing happened. Sparky fell apart alone in the dark trunk, crying and wiping the blood from the corner of his mouth. He must have, what?, passed out? Fallen asleep? Found enlightenment?

Died?

He felt very calm and wasn't surprised to push at the trunk of the car and feel it open easily. It was dark, wherever he and the car were, and quiet. The trunk swung wide open and Sparky waited. Nothing. Carefully he sat up and wiped at his face. Nothing. No blood. He and the car were in the garage. Stiffly, he rose and pulled himself out of the trunk. Sparky stretched and breathed. Nothing seemed to be broken. He stumbled a little but got into the house.

It wasn't night after all; just very dark in the garage with the lights out. He wandered around the house from room to room. He was alone. He was one. He didn't want to be one; he wanted to find Mummy. She wasn't in the front room or the kitchen or her room or anywhere. God, he needed a shower and something to eat. He wolfed down a sandwich in the kitchen, standing at the sink and idly not attaching importance to his racing thoughts.

His koan popped back into his thinking. Not one. Not two. Not not two. Then he thought of something and went back out to the garage. It was impossible, but then again he wasn't not two and never had been. He wasn't even surprised to find Mummy in the trunk of the car. She smiled up at him and he helped her out.

They went into the house and he made her some tea.

Cyrus doesn't even open her mouth until she's considered the consequences. How long? A year? A millennium?

It's all the same to Cyrus, still, she's not too keen to rush this. All is writhing chaos in every direction and the violence of erupting volcanoes and slamming tectonic plates has become a bit much. When she first twists around one full turn and brings all into existence, her first-ever experience is one of delight.

Well, look at this, would you? Clots of magnetically charged dust coalesce into masses that are pulled into globes that begin to spin in an intricate new dance, sort of but not quite obeying unacknowledged laws that confound even Cyrus. She floats amidst the new planets and marvels as some fire up into engines that emit light and heat, influencing the dance and complicating things for the dark globes, the ones that don't spark into stars.

Not one to see or even care about details, Cyrus is content to suspend herself and let the vast process do what it will. Small amusing frictions build up momentum and new levels of disruption arise and replicate themselves up and down the cosmic scale where there had once been endless dark and limitless silence.

What is birth after all but a rending of matter?

Each planet convulses itself and each star punishes anything that strays too close. Brilliance and bombast and the unmoored screeching of split apart atoms racket along Cyrus' elongated neural pathways and it becomes difficult to differentiate the creator from the created.

Who's running this show anyway?

Cyrus becomes restless and irritated. Just as she focuses on a particularly lovely pillar of cloud that is jettisoning newly spun stars some comet comes ripping through asteroid fields, smashing and gathering at the same time.

In vast concentric waves, this whole process is repeating itself with established stars casting unshadowed light for the new ones to attempt to ape and dark, shuddering planets to cluster about, confused and jockeying for good slots. At some far and unfathomable fringe, Cyrus' turn has lost none of its ferocious energy. Inertia, not yet invited to the party, hasn't yet asserted its indomitable sway and the chaos continues exploding in every direction.

Cyrus begins to ponder what another turn, in the other direction, might set into motion. Can all this be reversed and, if so, does she really want that? Up through a valley created by the formation of two new solar systems, comes something new and utterly unexpected yet somehow tantalizingly familiar. Carelessly knocking the struggling solar systems out of kilter, Cyrus swings around in a large arc to investigate. Only recently has she become aware of her own form amidst the violence, none of which is more than a satisfying itch and all of which delineates where she ends and her creation begins.

And so, what have we here?

It's deserving of serious investigation followed by long consideration of what to do next. As galaxies gain their foothold and the suggestions of gravity groove into shaky and constantly edited laws, Cyrus takes great delight in swimming around to bring that joyous tail into sight and then whipping it out in long, terrible sweeps that crush and reform trembling new star systems.

At every other level of perception, what was happening is catastrophic. For Cyrus, it is all fun and games. Somewhere out there in some quickly dissipated pool of melting black methane ice, a frantic scream for help goes up. And then another. And another. A rising chorus of protest and supplication sifts up through the smashing convulsions.

Even Cyrus begins to hear it and it grates terribly.

In an attempt to evade the insistent whining, she takes to long cruises up and down and to the furthest frontiers of her majestically unfolding universe. But she only gets so far when the temptation of her tail returns and she finds herself doing long, lazy spins, admiring the grace and reaching to brush her face against the tip. Just as she's on the cusp of some action, the shrieking of pre-sentient life finds her and off she goes again, violating all the struggling new laws of physics as she tears through the cosmos.

It's not that she gets tired exactly but boredom is truly universal and there comes a time when all this charging up and down and over and under just isn't that much fun anymore. The demands of mitochondrial DNA gathering in a hundred trillion patches of methane will not be denied. She slows at last and drifts for another several millennia, simply listening and observing. The laws that are trying to assert themselves are being constantly undermined by the inexorable push of all matter outward and in the midst of the maelstrom, the tiny and determined bits of what will become living, breathing, eating, fucking, shitting, lying, thinking, hunting, planning, designing, building, brick-laying, warring, harvesting, needing, giving, warning, dancing, scratching, confusing beings strive to gain a foothold.

As the whine crescendos up and withers down, Cyrus slides through the burgeoning universe in enormous circular spins, keeping that tail in sight and ponders an action that could have enormous and irreversible consequences.

Then she simply stops thinking and reaches across the galaxies' wide gap to firmly grasp her tail in her teeth. She doesn't delicately nip the tip; no, she fills her stupendously huge mouth with miles of tail and clamps down tightly, holding it firmly and feeling every shudder and pull along the full length of her invisible and powerful form.

In that moment, the cataclysmic expansion shudders into an elegant and neatly constructed dance of set actions and reactions. Whole new processes come into play and the stars' rule becomes absolute, gravity gains traction and in some forgettable tiny crevice on a planet easing into a happy, dependable orbit, two small molecules join and stayed joined.

Too late, Cyrus realizes her role now and can only spin into eternity, holding tightly to that tail lest all come undone.

It was a small thing, easy to miss, her virginity. What had all the carrying on been about, she wondered, smoothing her hand down the lower part of her belly but stopping before she actually touched there. He snored. Like some kind of animal, grunting and snorting in his sleep. Lerlene wasn't sleepy and she sure wished she could call Kimmy up and talk this over. But Kimmy was gone off to the west coast with her Marine.

Lerlene eased herself out of the narrow bed. It was always stuffy in this place and it smelled off, not bad really but off. She could find work, she was sure of it, then they could move into something decent. It'd be nice if they could afford one of those great new double-wides like her Uncle Steve had bought last year.

Maybe once Aiden got his green card now that they were married he'd be able to get back to work. He said he'd worked construction before. He might even be able to get into the union; then they'd be set. Dream on.

She fumbled around in the dark for the light switch in the bathroom. It wasn't where it was supposed to be, so she tried the other side of the door. There. Quick like, she pushed the door closed so the light wouldn't wake this stranger she'd gone and married. Until she got a better feel for where things stood, it was just better to play it safe. He did seem like a decent sort. He'd been careful so as not to hurt her when they were doing it; that had eased her mind some. Mommie could have been wrong.

She'd just pulled down her panties and sat on the toilet when she heard someone knocking on the back door. What the...? Whoever it was, they were pounding that door loud enough to wake the dead and it still took Aiden the longest time to answer it. Lerlene didn't need to pee so bad now and quietly rose, pulled her panties up and went to listen by the closed door. She thought she could make out two other voices besides Aidan's Irish roil that still had her knees going floppy.

It felt like the speakers were keeping their voices down. Did they know she was here? How? Lerlene held her breath and crouched by the door to see if she could make out a word here or there. Whoever they were, they weren't speaking like Aiden did. They were locals.

Then one of the voices got louder and Lerlene was so shocked she nearly fell over.

It was her Uncle Steve and he sounded pissed. Big surprise there; this was exactly why she'd made sure not to tell anyone in her family about marrying Aiden. Except Sissy Marie who'd been snooping through Lerlene's things and found the marriage license. Lerlene should have known Sissy Marie wouldn't keep her big mouth shut.

"What's going on out here?" Lerlene put on her boldest voice, stepping out into the room.

Oh, Jesus, would you look at that, Lerlene thought. Sagging next to Uncle Steve was her dear old Dad, the son of a bitch who'd stopped paying child support when she was ten and Sissy Marie was in kindergarten. Both men reared back like they were going to hit someone or some stupid shit like that. Typical.

"Well, would ya look at what we got here, husband mine."

Lerlene linked her arm through Aiden's slack one and smiled. Now everyone was just going to stand here and look like idiots. Fine with her. She just continued to smile and let them squirm. If Aiden needed to squirm too, well that was his problem.

"What's the matter with you, girl? Go put some clothes on! We come to take you home where you belong." This from Uncle Steve because the Good Lord knew her lousy deadbeat father had best keep that trap of his shut.

"I am home."

"Yeah, Lerlene is my wife and this is our home." Aiden spoke up. Finally.

Aiden seemed to be gathering his wits which was welcome at this point. He was a big, strapping man and those two stupid hillbillies were not going to just drag her out of here like they apparently thought they could. Again, typical.

"You been drinking?" Lerlene already knew the answer to that one and both her father and uncle knew she knew. "What in the hell is wrong with you two?" Now she let go of Aiden and stepped forward, hissing in fury. "You," at the man who supposedly sired her, "since when do you give a tinker's dam about what I do or who I do it with?" She all but spit at his feet but it is, as has already been established, her home and she's been raised better than to be messing up her own place.

"And you," this to big, bad Uncle Steve who was backing away, "what business do you have coming by our home in the middle of the night trying to start trouble? You both do realize I'm 17 years old and can marry any damned man I please, right?"

"Gentlemen, I'm going to ask you to leave now." Aiden, bless him, seemed to think this would work. He genuinely believed these two ninnies would just up and leave because he'd asked them nicely.

Well, Uncle Steve knew when he was beat but now all of a sudden it was that skinny, old asshole, her "father" who was going to get all righteous. She could see it coming, him working up a good fit to throw. Fuck. That.

"You got two goddamned seconds to get the hell out of our home or I'm calling the police and you," rounding soundly on her father, "you got some nerve showing up here like this. Get your skinny ass back to whatever hole you been hiding in the past nine years."

Looking like two whipped hounds, the two men departed. And now, here's Aiden looking at Lerlene with something new going on in those big, hazel eyes. She takes him by the hand and leads him back towards the bedroom. This bride is home.

Branch Into Bone

What Trees Know That We Don't

Tangled and crossed and crashing into each other in this riotous wind, my limbs disobey my brain and even in there twigs strain to reach each other, throwing defiant sparks across the stubborn gaps.

I know this stuff; I invented this stuff. Why can't I remember? It's right here, right on the tip of my.....leaf?

My root system is deep but the wind tonight, it's strong. I flex and grip and hang on. I've made it through worse nights. So had you. But where are you now? I sweep the bare ground next to me with low slung branches that chatter and shake. Another gust slams into my mass. Is that rain? Snow maybe? I never feel the cold, just the aloneness. The wind had less purchase on my foliage when you stood next to me.

From seedlings on, here we were, rooted and together. Others sprouted, rose, thrived, shot towards the sky and, one by one, they were cut away, withered by disease, pissed on by one too many dogs, chewed by deer and then it was just us. You and me. Mighty, soaring and impervious. Or so we thought. Remember how we'd laugh on nights like this?

Here she is again; why she only comes out on the wild nights is a mystery. I never see her face, she wears that hood always. She's been coming out here for a very long time, for her kind anyway it's a long time. Years. She always comes alone. I might be attributing thoughts, insight to her that she's incapable of, but I like to think that she misses you, too.

Her warm little presence under there is comforting. She can't protect me. She didn't protect you. Still, tonight I'm glad she's here.

Marie feels for her key but can't imagine why it matters. It isn't like she's going back. There's nothing to go back to. The emptiness of the house she left is almost violent. All those years of running up and down those stairs, fetching this and carrying that, wiping another snotty little nose and soothing another fretting little soul.

Others who grew up around here fled as soon as they could and why not? There's nothing here. But with her first pregnancy, her roots were sunk. She wasn't going anywhere. There was always someone needing taken care of. First, it was good to have her mother's help, but then her mother needed mothering, too. Daddy died and that actually made things a little easier in some ways.

There was a patch in there when things were good. Right? Marie eases right on down the well-trod path of checking the past for clues of happiness, of contentment. Her husband had once smiled when he saw her. But with the birth of each next child, his misery and resentment grew, seeking comfort roughly in her flesh and begetting yet more of his own special brand of hell. More mouths to feed. There was a time when they both cursed their plenitude.

No more. All are gone.

He was the first to go. Just didn't come home from work one night and that was it. Then the horrors began. Accidents, illness, poverty and finally the State stepping in and scooping away the last three confused little kids.

It's cold enough out here.

Ridiculously, she pulls her coat tight around her as she huddles in down at the base of the trunk of the remaining oak. She leans against the hard trunk and tells death to get it over with; she's ready. Right. As if she'll get an even break in dying. Life was nearly impossible; why should death be different?

She steadies herself and is surprised that the bark is warm, giving. The sighs above her vibrate with a kindness that can't just be the wind. She reaches up and grasps a hand; yes, it is a hand. Around her, branches coalesce into arms and someone tall and strong and patient reaches down to prepare the ground.

Eventually, the authorities come out to claim the house, to bulldoze it and let the forest return. No one notices that there are two oaks out back again. This part of the county isn't really up for development, too swampy and too far from the interstate. In time the strip malls and gas stations will encroach, but for now, two root systems are entwined deep under the ground and the wind can only tug and howl.

Ground and sky bracket two growing trees.

"I hate it when that fat spic runs the vacuum cleaner right outside of my room first thing every morning." Mr. Bluebird is, hands down, the most annoying 'guest' in this sad excuse for a hotel. "Can't she jest say no to the Mickey D's? Hell, I can't hardly get past her in the hallway."

Marjean's enjoying the breeze coming in the front door; smells a little like rain. There's some good, old Motown playing on the radio and she's got a cup of Brenda's excellent coffee. Be nice if that new one would sleep in once in awhile or at least keep his nasty bigoted yap shut.

Isn't it just a blessing that Arnaud never finishes up the night paperwork and now she has that to focus on? As Mr. Bluebird lumbers by on his way out to the porch she thinks that he has his nerve. He's three hundred pounds if he's an ounce.

Then, bang, and she's aching to be back in Atlanta. It's been two years since she gave in and moved down here to Gulfport with Frank. He loves it here and it's nice enough that he's happy. It got to be such a trial, how miserable he was in the city, always wanting to go out driving in the country and stopping at every 'for sale' sign they passed. When he got the chance to transfer, well, it wasn't as if Marjean had any kind of great career going or anything. Most of her people are still down around here. She wants a city; there's New Orleans right on down the road.

"Jesus, it's quiet here. Drives me nuts." Mr. Bluebird is back. He's got his morning paper and settles into one of the sagging, leatherette couches.

Mr. Bluebird retired down here after driving bus up north for forty years and his hometown paper is delivered daily. His boy lives over in Mobile; doesn't come around but once a week though. What a shocker. Old Bluebird always goes straight to the obits to see who he's outlived today. It doesn't seem to faze him much that the paper is three days old. For the next ten minutes the only sounds in the already too-warm lobby are rustling papers, the radio and the occasional swish of a car on the road out front. There. Marjean's got it straight now and neatens up the pile, fitting it into the night slot.

"How can you stand it here?" Bluebird's voice makes her jump. "You weren't born around here. I can tell."

"It's nice here." Marjean says, keeping it short.

"Yea, if you got a room temperature IQ. It's a goddamned morgue without the formaldehyde."

"Oh, there you are, Mister Bluebird!" Miss Jameson trips into the lobby as if balancing on bound feet. "You don't want to be late for breakfast, now do you?"

"Wouldn't kill me to miss a meal or two." Nevertheless, he begins heaving himself up out of the creaking sofa. "Nice talking with you, Missus Baxter." Gaining his feet, he pauses and turns back to Marjean. "You need to work on your sincerity. Either that or quit lying."

Marjean won't glare as he stumps out of the lobby with Miss Jameson attached to his flank like one of those suckerfish you see on sharks on National Geographic specials. Then, as they turn past the stairway, she automatically pulls a bland, professional smile into place just in case either of them look over towards her. They don't.

The day gets darker and Marjean notices how people begin to kind of creep through the lobby. The elderly ladies cluck and tuck wadded tissues into their sleeves. The old men sniff the still air like saggy, tired hounds; then they shake their heads and retreat to the parlor where Judge Judy rules. No one is foolish enough to bring up names like Camille, Andrew and Hilda. This is not superstition; it's just common courtesy.

The Gulfview Plaza had been a grand place back in the day; although in those more genteel times it was called The Mayfair Hotel. Set a good twenty miles inland, the new name is a lame attempt to draw the tourist trade. This owner's version of antebellum sophistication includes heavy velvet swags that cut the light in the lobby. The carpet is a conference room busy print: fleur de lis stack up in a dizzy, diagonal sweep.

The trick name hasn't really worked to get tourists in the door. Gulfport still draws its share of snowbirds, but they've either got time-shares or stay in places that actually have views of the gulf. Most of the guests at The Plaza are monthly paying residents whose rents are subsidized by this or that government program. In the fusty old novels that Marjean's mother favors, they would have been called pensioners. Here and now, they are just old people and mental cases who forget to take their meds.

"Man, there was almost no better way to fuck up everyone's day than to have a second wheelchair waiting at the stop." It's dinnertime and Mr. Bluebird is holding forth from his place at the head of one of the tables. "I mean, yeah, it's too bad an' all when someone's stuck in a wheelchair, but I gotta tell you, I could feel it all around me onna bus. Everyone hated it when I gotta stop and spend all that time dicking around with the lift. That ADA was one misguided piece of legislation; let me tell you." He waves his forkful of roast pork and gravy at the rest of the table. "An', ya know, most of them cripples are fat! They must really build them chairs to last. I seen some of them women had to tip the scales at 300 easy. The whole damned bus would list to the side when I'd get 'em onto the lift."

Marjean usually has dinner here with the guests after clocking off her shift. Frank's never home til whenever; no point in rushing home to sit around by herself. That old gasbag Bluebird is unbelievable but she keeps her own mouth shut. It's enough to listen to the other guests. Miss Jameson, now she sees the sun rising behind Bluebird's head every morning; he can't say a wrong thing to her way of thinking. But others mutter to themselves, mostly at the other tables. Old Bluebird will light into anyone who disagrees with him, and it's just easier to let him yammer on.

Marjean never sits at his table though she gets quite an earful from the gallery. Sometimes it's all she can do to not laugh out loud. Little, bitty Missus Myers is the best. She'd been a grammar teacher and then principle at Francis Xavier Elementary for more years than anyone could count and she knows what to do with that vinegar on her tongue.

"Hope Bluebelly stayed on the other side of the bus when he was operating that lift, otherwise that bus would have gone over for sure." Some of the other ladies at the table titter and cover their mouths with their napkins. Missus Myer's sharp eyes crease and she raises her eyebrows in Marjean's direction. "Now then, our Mrs. Baxter, she is a true gentlewoman and a professional. I ought to be ashamed of myself, carrying on like this in your hearing, Mrs. Baxter."

Marjean dips her head ever so slightly. It wouldn't do to be seen as agreeing with one guest regarding another's shortcomings. Mr. Bluebird is droning on over at the other table and Marjean notices that there are more empty places over there tonight. But his stalwarts remain; a covey of timidly bitter old fools who nod and guffaw, but never come up with anything themselves. Good thing this place never gets filled up. There's always room for other guests to avoid Bluebird.

Marjean had been on the desk the day Bluebird arrived with his silent daughter in tow. The look on that poor woman's face said it all. Mr. Angelo Bluebird had responded to forced retirement by having a major stroke. Therapy had left him looking only slightly lopsided, his thick lips almost meeting on the left side and just a bit of a droop to that left eye. He scanned the lobby critically and gestured for the girl to set his bag down.

"My boy call? The name's Bluebird and save the jokes."

Marjean decided not to waste time with empty welcoming and pulled out the call log. "Yes, sir, Mr. Dante Bluebird called last week to arrange your room. Would you like to have your bags taken up? Lunch is being served in the dining room."

"If I wanted to know about lunch. I'd have asked." He turned to the mortified daughter. "Where the fuck is Dante?"

The girl stammered, first going red and then white, managing to choke out something about Dante having a meeting and that he planned to come by later to see that his father was settled in all right.

"Meeting, huh? 'Bout time that lazy shit got off his ass and started making things happen. What kinda meeting?" Almost immediately he backed off from that, "Oh, never mind, Belinda. Just see that my stuff is taken up. I'm gonna have some lunch." And with that Marjean was left looking at Belinda who managed a shrug but not much in the way of a smile.

Marjean's pulling on her coat when the phone rings. Arnaud answers it and then gestures to her.

"Hey, dollface, where you at?" Frank could be so clueless.

Marjean should resist, and if she were a better person she might, but in her driest tone asks, "I don't know. What number did you dial?"

"You know what I mean!"

"I'm on my way out the door now." She doesn't have the energy. "What's up?"

"This storm is set to hit sometime tomorrow and they're making noises about evacuation along the coast." Frank is a geologist whose computer models predict where best to drill for oil. He spends more time out on the drilling platforms in the gulf than Marjean's happy about, but there's nothing for it. It's not like he has to be out there, either, but it makes him feel like a real man or something. At least he's in for this storm.

"Did you call my mom yet?" Marjean's mother, Carla, is pushing 90 and won't be budged from the tiny house she'd been born in down in the Gentilly neighborhood of New Orleans. Against all odds, the old place has survived Katrina and so has Carla. Her kids might be scattered to the four winds but Carla Marie Leveaux is not leaving New Orleans except in a box.

"No answer. I left a message. We might need to get outta Dodge."

"You eat yet?" Marjean says; everyone was so jumpy about storms anymore.

"Yea, got a sandwich at Hurley's. You already et, right?"

"I'll see you in a few." Marjean looks over to Arnaud as she hangs up. "Frank says they're talking evacuation again. Better keep an eye on the weather channel." Arnaud nods and reaches for the remote to the little black and white behind the desk.

Marjean's almost to the door when Bluebird stumps into the lobby with several of his birds in tow. All she needs to hear is the word 'Jews' and she's on her way out the door with her coat only half on. One of the little old men, a new guy, throws a pleading look at Marjean, but she's fresh out of lifelines tonight and can only muster a sympathetic shrug before making her own escape. Arnaud remains focused on the little television. The poor old guy is on his own.

The rain comes in the night. Not a lot of wind yet, just sheets of rain; rain you can't see through. Marjean's glad all over again that Frank is in tonight and, even though they've both already eaten, she makes a little meal. She even finds and opens the last bottle of dago red that Frank's brother sent from his vineyard in upstate New York. The clatter of the rain on the tin roof of the back porch becomes deafening, so she closes the back door and takes the food into the living room where Frank is, where else?, in front of the computer.

She kisses the back of his neck and barely notices that he doesn't respond. Marjean sets his food on the table beside the computer desk, it's where he usually eats, then settles into the big wingback chair by the window. The street lights are ripply smears in the rain. No traffic to speak of. Sipping the heavy, red wine, she clicks the TV on and turns to the weather channel. This gets Frank's attention and he's surprised to find food has magically appeared.RED. They eat and watch the latest Doppler images.

The storm had been downgraded to a tropical depression after crossing south Florida but has regrouped out there in the Gulf. Marjean's doubly glad Frank's not out on one of the platforms. There's been no word from her mother; but Marjean's not worried. She's got three brothers down near there and Mommy's house has been through some hundred and twenty years of hurricanes. Stubborn old bird'll survive Armageddon.

"Nothing from Carla?" Frank's just making conversation. He knows Mommy.

"Not a word. Marcus and Antoine'll be over there by now."

"Why don't you call Denise?"

"You think?" Marjean asked.

"Sure, you know she's not gonna be trailing after Antoine. No point in dragging the kids over there."

"That's true. Never have seen anyone less interested in her grandkids than Mommy."

"She got her fill with ya'll. Don't blame her," Frank said, grinning.

"Watch it, bub." Marjean mimes throwing her spoon at him but reaches for the phone. She dials, listens and then hangs up. "Lines are all tied up."

"Or down."

"Don't say that!"

"Don't worry. Ain't no storm mean enough to face Carla Marie down."

"I'm not worried."

Frank gets up and comes over to her chair, tucking himself in next to her. It's good not to have to say every damned little thing out loud.

The rain is steady in the morning as Marjean pulls out of the driveway. Frank's been gone for hours but had set the alarm fifteen minutes early so they could snuggle before he left. The radio's all about the weather and the evacuation. Marjean was able to get through to Carla Marie this morning. She didn't waste her breath trying to get Mommy to evacuate, just made sure she had plenty of bottled water and that there was gas in the generator. And that she had shells for the shotgun. She pulls into the lot next to the Plaza and cuts the engine off. She needs a minute.

"We got us a full house, Marjean." Mr. Tanner, the manager, greets her the minute she walks in the front door.

"No kidding." The lobby is packed with milling people and piles of luggage and blankets. Marjean wonders about the universal need to bring blankets along in almost any kind of emergency. Mostly these are folks from nearer the water, who don't have cars or another way further inland although some just didn't want to be sitting out on the interstate waiting for the storm to get worse.

Tanner comes over and drops his voice, "See what you can do with that asshole bus driver. These people are jumpy enough, Lord knows."

"Got some duct tape?"

Tanner laughs and walks off, leaving Marjean to hang up her wet slicker and get to work. The desk is a mess; it's a good thing Marjean likes Arnaud. She's just getting things straightened out when the front door crashes open and more wet, cranky people cram into the lobby. Marjean gets real busy and loses track of time. Residents poke their heads out of their rooms, get another look at the chaos and retreat. Mrs. Devlin and her kitchen staff do the impossible and put a plate of food into every hand.

As Marjean rushes upstairs to help a porter clear out a back storage room, it occurs to her that there's been no sign of Bluebird today. Then, just as she turns to go back downstairs, she hears that dissatisfied rumble. Maybe he's just got one of his usual victims cornered but she's got to check. No such luck. There he is, blocking the hallway and scolding a middle-aged black man. Marjean stomach shrinks into a sour ball the size of a walnut.

"What the hell are you fools thinking of, living on the coast like that? What do you think is *gonna* happen every hurricane season? And then, you're gonna go right back on down there, wanting the government to fix everything when you find everything you own is flattened and lost."

He's underestimated his target. This isn't some frail, old grandfather.

"You don't know me. You don't know where I live. And you will get out of my way, you fat sonuvabitch!" The other man is exhibiting astonishing restraint to Marjean's way of thinking as she bears down on the scene of the crime. "And while we're at it, fat man, it appears that you live right here along side of the rest of us fools, am I right?"

She's almost there, but not — quite...

"Why you mouthy n-" Bluebird suddenly appears to get a clue as to where he is and who he's talking to the way he bites off that word.

Marjean sees the man clenching his fists and gets to the end of the hallway right at that moment.

"I am so sorry, Mr. — " Pause.

"Linders." He's tight and ready.

Without even looking at Bluebird, Marjean insinuates herself between the two men and makes room for Mr. Linders to get to the stairs. He glares at Bluebird and Marjean hears the rattly breath being pulled. Snapping her head around, she fixes Bluebird with the look and is mildly surprised when it works. The fat man stays silent and Marjean gets her angry guest down to the lobby. What to say now?

"Mr. Linders, please accept our apology for Mr. Bluebird's unacceptable behavior. May we offer your room gratis?" She'll just have to make it right with Tanner. Linders is still furious and now there's only one target available: herself. She will take Bluebird to pieces and leave him on the ash pile out back later but now she composes herself and waits.

"I could close you down. I could sue this place and own every cheesy piece of fake velvet in here; you know that? And *you*, what the hell are you doing working in a place that allows that kind of garbage? You think you have to take that shit just because the boss gives you a paycheck! It's not 1958 anymore, woman, wake up!"

Secretly, shamefully, she's grateful Linders can't know she's married to a white man.

"Mister Linders, sir, please don't give our Mrs. Baxter such grief. The burden this poor woman bears for the rest of us is not to be believed, sir."

And suddenly here's Missus Myers, standing like a Citadel cadet next to Marjean.

"The old fool you had the misfortune of crossing paths with upstairs, Mr. Angelo Bluebird, is a relic and something of a laughingstock here. We tolerate the ignorant SOB in a way that we're aware he'd never tolerate any of us."

Marjean watches the expression on Linders' face as Missus Myers leads him over to one of the sagging couches. The ferocious lines between his eyes have eased; he's listening. Seeing her opening, Marjean makes a fast trip to the kitchen for tea. When she gets back, there's Linders laughing with Missus Myers like they're old friends.

"Mrs. Baxter, I owe you an apology. That kind of stupidity sends me into a blind rage every time. But taking it out on you is as unacceptable as anything that came out of the old bigot's mouth," He skooches over a bit, "Please join us?"

"Much as I'd love that, I'm afraid I'm on the desk and there are still a lot of people to get settled." She pauses briefly, then sets the tea tray down and extends her hand. "Thank you, Mr. Linders, you are a real gentleman."

Tanner isn't happy about offering a free room, but Marjean figures he's angrier at old Bluebird than at her. She gets real busy again and sort of forgets about the storm outside. Marjean, like anyone born and raised up in this part of the world, respects the power of weather but knows you can't let it get the better of you. You take your precautions; you don't be foolish and then you get on with stuff. Frank's been checking in regular; he's good that way.

"Look, babe, I don't want you out in that. You sit tight and I'll come by after I finish up here." Frank never sounds worried no matter what's coming out of his mouth.

"Ok. Tanner says we can bunk here in the lobby if you want." Marjean says.

"Big of him, but this one's gonna have to throw more than 100 mile per hour winds to keep us off the road." Frank loved it when there was an actual, practical reason to drive his big, yellow Hummer.

"Honeypie, have you looked outdoors lately?"

"I don't need to; I'm surrounded by state of the art monitoring gizmos. Wind speed's only up to 80 mph. She's gonna weenie out."

"From your lips to the ears of God." Marjean sees Tanner hurrying over. "Look, don't rush on my account. We're good here and I'd rather you stayed in that bunker at least until we get to the eye, ok?"

"Maybe I should just bring you back here."

"I'll call." Marjean hopes he'll catch her tone.

"Good enough, dollface. Later." He does.

She hangs up and faces the manager. Tanner is never particularly comfortable in his own skin and this afternoon he's hopped up good. He's wanting to pitch his voice low but the wind is howling right outside the plywood up over the windows and finally, he just has to speak up to be heard.

"We're gonna need to double the residents up to make room. I got the boys setting up cots, three to a room." He's pausing now, staring down at his shoes like a kid. "Guess we can't really put anyone in with Bluebird. Right?"

"*Oh you best believe it, boss.*" This doesn't make it out of Marjean's mouth but Tanner gets the gist.

As if prompted by some amateur stage director, the door crashes open and another gang of wet, crabby people arrive. Tanner's panicking. Isn't this just marvelous? This is what happens when corporate promotes someone from out of state who's only used to dealing with conventions and unions.

"Look, I'll take care of it." Marjean's already on the move and Tanner's just going to have to take the desk. She heads into the back parlor and there's Bluebird's gang looking to be about as animated as an empty balloon without him there blowing hot air. Where is the son of a bitch? Probably holed up in his room with a chair propped under the door knob lest management tries to foist any niggers or spics on him.

Hours later, with the wind really whaling and most everyone bedded down, Marjean finally gets to call Frank. He's still at work.

"Dollface, don't even try going out there, k?"

"I won't if you won't." Marjean's too damned tired to go anywhere.

"This isn't looking good." Frank, the master of understatement, actually sounds unsettled.

"It's gonna hit New Orleans, isn't it?"

"Looking like."

"I been trying to get through to my brothers; they may need to get Mommy out of there."

"I'm going down before it gets worse."

Marjean shakes her head and stretches her mouth wide open without making any noise. She can feel Frank waiting. There is nothing for it; she can't leave here and he can. "Thank you. And, look you, stay in touch, hear?"

"Count on it, babe, and please do not leave there."

"Right."

"Get some sleep. I'll call when I get down there, let you know how things are."

Like she's going to be able to sleep. "Ok, then, I love you."

"I love you, too, dollface."

And he is gone.

Marjean sits up, surprised that she slept, and reaches for her cell phone. Nothing. He said he'd call. He'll call. The roar outside has steadied. The desk is piled up with Arnaud's undone work and he's over asleep on the loveseat in the corner. He left the little black and white TV on. Marjean doesn't want to turn the volume up and leans down to hear what's going on now. Mandatory evacuation down there in Louisiana.

She flips her phone open again and tries Frank's number. Nothing. May as well clean up that mess on the desk. Time is congealing and going static. After what feels like hours, she looks over and finds that less than forty minutes have passed.

When that top step squeaks under Bluebird's bulk, she grits her teeth. He glares at her and says not one word. She knows that after the scene with Linders, Tanner had a little talk with Mr. Bluebird but doesn't know exactly what was said. Since then, though, the old bus driver has stopped talking. Let him sulk.

"It's like having a smoking volcano stumping around the place, isn't it?" Missus Myers comes over to the desk to see if the mail's run. It hasn't, of course, and both women know it.

"It is what it is, Missus Myers." Marjean shrugs and works to keep a neutral tone without coming off as rude.

"Amanda."

"Excuse me?"

"Call me Amanda, please."

"Uh, well, yes, if you'd like — Amanda." Marjean is not comfortable with this but doesn't see a way to refuse without offending. The older woman has always been forthcoming and friendly but now she acts as if the two are co-conspirators. Unable to figure out how to re-establish the former boundary between guest and employee, Marjean settles for hiding in her work. Amanda is not put off.

"He's going to blow, you know."

"Missus — Amanda, please don't take this the wrong way, but I have a lot of work to do and...," Marjean pauses. Missus Myers is not stupid.

"Oh, dear, Mrs. Baxter, I'm sorry. You're right, of course. Please forgive me for a meddling old lady, out here gossiping and carrying on."

She leaves and it isn't lost on either woman that Marjean has remained 'Mrs. Baxter'. Silence returns to the lobby and Marjean resists the temptation to go the kitchen for another cup of coffee. Any more caffeine and there's no telling what could come out of her mouth next.

She's not going to be sucked in again. Making friends with guests is always a mistake, no matter how friendly and smart they are.

By midmorning this one's given all it's got. As storms went, it wasn't all that but then again Marjean and Frank aren't trees, are they? Stepping out of the Gulfview in the morning, Marjean sees that just about every tree and shrub in every direction was flattened. It's going to take weeks to clean up around here.

In her pocket she feels her cell phone vibrate. It's Frank and he puts Mommy on the phone. Carla keeps it short; she's got some clearing up to do and has food for Frank to be bringing back. Marjean listens, sagging a little in relief.

Old Bluebird is a tough one all right. Weeks pass and he holds fast; glaring at everyone and saying nothing. Dante must be taking the brunt of it, Marjean thinks, judging from the dark circles under his sad eyes that get darker and deeper each time he brings his father back from their Sunday afternoon out. Looking at Dante, pretty and slightly pudgy, you could see the younger Angelo Bluebird and Marjean thinks that maybe the old jerk wasn't always a fat, hateful old racist.

Right. Once he was a young, pudgy racist.

On a Sunday right before Thanksgiving, Dante's SUV pulls up out front and the two men get out and come up on the porch.

"Hear this one?" It's the first time Marjean's heard Mr. Bluebird's voice in weeks. She's right by the door, getting her jacket and she freezes, eavesdropping in spite of herself. The two have settled into rocking chairs right outside the door and Mr. Bluebird continues.

"Why does Mike Tyson cry during sex?"

Dante says nothing. Maybe he nods.

"Mace'll do that to you!" Bluebird explodes into his spitty, guttural laughter and something inside Marjean pops. Setting her jaw, she pulls on her coat. Banging the door open she stops to glare at the suddenly choked-off Bluebird. The two lock eyes and Dante shifts nervously.

"What do you call it when an Italian has one arm shorter than the other?" Marjean asks like it's a real question.

Mr. Bluebird blinks in surprise. Marjean, loving the confusion in his eyes, lets him wait it out for three solid beats.

"A speech impediment."

And just that quick, both Bluebird and Marjean are laughing their heads off. Now Dante's looking bewildered.

Unfortunately, after this, Mr. Bluebird becomes her best friend. It's not what she intended. It's not what she wants. And no amount of professional courtesy and distance gets through to the old fart. He's no Amanda Myers with an ear set to hear another person's discomfort. Waddling importantly across the lobby, he slaps a thick hand onto the counter and inquires as to Marjean's health. She shifts and avoids eye contact. She calls him Mr. Bluebird and he calls her Marjean even though she never told him her name.

At dinner he adopts the practice of calling over to where Marjean is sitting, seeking her opinion about the Crimson Tide's chances or the weather tomorrow. Wearily, she shakes her head and is aware of Amanda Myers' watchful eyes.

There's always some point in the meal where Bluebird just has to go off on some godawful rant or, worse, crowing about how well one of the "bucks" of the "his" team did, winning him a "shit ton" of money.

The tension around the room is as palpable as it is familiar. No one likes this and no one says a word about it. No one challenges him. Everyone sits with their heads down pushing their food around their plates and feeling bad. Something clicks in Marjean's head and suddenly here it all comes. She knows this is a stupid move and can't stop the words, the stones from falling out of her mouth.

"Mr. Bluebird, I wonder if it would be too much to ask you to please watch your mouth, sir?"

Bluebird stops in mid-guffaw and stares at Marjean.

"I can only speak for myself, you understand, sir, but sitting here listening to you carry on about "coons" and "niggers" and "spics", turning the word Jew into a slur, I don't know, sir, but I'm thinking you certainly wouldn't care for it were Arnaud and I to begin referring to your grandchildren as greasy, little wops." She stops, her face is burning and her hands are clenched under the stiff, white table cloth.

No one is eating. Everyone is silently watching Bluebird's swollen face getting more and more red.

"Does it never occur to you that I find your racist blithering to be so offensive that I want to throw up?"

Bluebird is spluttering now.

"But...you ain't black, Marjean."

"What the *hell* difference would that make if I weren't? And you might want to check in with my Mama if you're going to make that kind of assumption."

If she says one more word, Marjean's going to either throw something at Mr. Bluebird or burst into tears. She leaves. She just gets up, throws her napkin on her chair and walks out of the dining room without looking at anyone. Thank goodness no one follows her.

"Frank. I think I might have lost my job today." She's home to their empty house and calling Frank at the office. She listens and gets a beer from the fridge.

"Well, I — remember that guest I told you about, the jerk from Cleveland, used to drive a bus?" Listens. Opens the beer and gets a glass. "Yep, that's the one. No, sure, go ahead and get it, I'll wait."

Snaps on the television and mutes it, reads the closed captioning for the MacNeil Newshour and waits. She knows Frank's ridiculously busy but has no one else to talk to about this. No way is she calling her mother.

"Yeah, I'm here."

Franks is one of the world's great listeners.

"Well, I lost it with him tonight. I went off on him at dinner."

Listens, sips the beer.

"Another load of crap about 'coons' and 'nappy-headed brats.'"

Waits.

"Yea, that's what he said all right. Christ, Frank, I'm sorry."

Listens.

"No, no one said anything. I guess if no one calls me tonight, I'll just go on in tomorrow and find out."

Waits, changes the channel; it's pledge drive time.

"You'll be pretty late then tonight?"

Catches the end of the weather report on channel eight. Rain tomorrow.

"Ok, no. I won't wait up."

Listens.

"No. No, I won't worry. I know I'll find work all right."

He's being as much help as he can and Marjean knows it. It's not his fault that it's not anywhere near enough.

"Ok, sweetheart. Thanks for listening."

Waits.

"Don't work too hard."

Listens.

"I love you, too. Bye."

And she's alone. Sure, sure, she'll find work. But the sick knot in her stomach won't ease. Maybe another beer. Is this why she's kept her mouth shut all these years? Is this why she stopped Frank from saying anything to those assholes on their wedding day? What good is standing up to the idiocy if all it does is to lose her a job and make her feel like shit? Shouldn't she feel some small triumph at the look on his face tonight?

Checking the fridge, Marjean finds leftovers from last night's carry out that Frank brought home and five more bottles of beer. Screw it. She's not hungry and she is lonely and scared. She takes all five beers and stretches out on the couch, flipping through the channels without seeing or hearing what's on. Halfway through the third beer she's not so scared and is starting to get a little angry. Why should she be expected to just take that kind of crap? Because she's a good girl, that's why; because she's a woman. If she were a man, she could have punched Bluebird right in his big, fat gut and that would have been that.

Finishing the fourth beer, Marjean's really mad (yeah, she's what Frank calls a real lightweight when it comes to the sauce). She reaches for the last beer and eyes the telephone. They can't fire her. Not if she quits. And — hey, they can't say squat because she can call the EEOP and the NAACP and the ACLU and she'll just sue their ass, that's what she'll do, dammit. Getting up, she sways over to the phone pausing to take a very macho slug off her beer and almost falling. Just as she regains her balance and reaches for the phone, it rings. Shocked, she falls for sure this time and lands in Frank's computer chair.

"He — hello?"

"Mrs. Baxter, Marjean?" It's Missus Myers.

Marjean holds the receiver away from her ear and gazes at it in wonder before putting it back to the side of her head.

"How — how'd you get my number?"

"I'm sorry to bother you at home, especially after what happened here earlier, but I thought you should know that Bluebelly went and had another stroke tonight....but, listen, Marjean, it's *not* anything to do with you or what you said." Marjean's gone totally blank. "Marjean? Marjean, are you still there? Are you all right?"

"I — uh."

"Marjean, you sound funny. Are you sure you're all right?"

"Missus Myers, look I — well, I just — I mean...," Marjean pulls in a long, ragged breath, "*Why* did you call me?"

"Why, Marjean Baxter, you are drunk as a lord!"

"Uh, and so what?"

"Bless your heart, woman, I am so relieved. I was beginning to wonder if there was a human being in there after all."

"Fuck off."

Click. There, enough of all of them. Oh shit, Bluebird's gonna go off and die now and it's all her fault. She crawls back over to the couch, kicking over that last beer and huddles up, rocking and weeping until she passes out.

Marjean hasn't felt this bad in ages. Between the hangover, the pounding rain on the roof of the car and the dread of what she'll be facing when she gets to the Gulfview, she just wishes she could have a stroke herself. Arnaud's pickup is still in the lot; not a good sign but what the hell did she expect anyway? He gives her his most soulful look when she comes in, shaking her umbrella and inwardly hunkering down, getting ready for the blow. When she turns from hanging her slicker she's surprised to see Dante Bluebird approaching her with his hand out.

"Mrs. Baxter, I hope you're all right." His grip is surprisingly warm and firm. "I asked Mr. Tanner if I could speak with you. I hope that's all right?"

"Oh, I — , Mr. Bluebird, I'm so awfully sorry about your father. Is he going to be ok? Do you have any news?" Marjean keeps her mouth and legs moving even as her heart sinks. Yea, she knows Tanner'll want to 'talk' to her all right.

"Pop's in bad shape, but the doctors back up north had warned him about this what with his weight and the way he drank and smoked and all. We all knew it was just a matter of time, y'see?" He's leading Marjean over to sit down his eyes never leaving her face. He looks real worried and Marjean figures she must be a sight. They sit down and when Dante reaches for her hand she doesn't pull it away even though she wants to.

"I bet I've apologized for Pop more than you can imagine and you probably have a pretty good idea what I'm talking about. See," he pauses and averts his eyes for a moment, "Pop wasn't always this bad. He's never been an easy one. He was a tough father and kind of a mean guy to Mom but it wasn't until after that first stroke that he got so — obnoxious." Another pause. "Anyway, I'm just real, real sorry about the crappy things

                    T.REMINGTON

he said and for the way he behaved around here. I'm sorry you had to be in the line of fire the way you were."

Marjean's mouth feels like it's full of stones again. She can't move her arms and her mouth seems stuck. Somewhere deep in the back of her throat a furious voice is demanding to know what difference this lame ass apology is supposed to make. It's a voice she's quelled all her life. She's quelling it now. What would be helped by more anger, more mean words? Summoning vestiges of dignity, she gently removes her hand from Dante's.

"Thank you, Mr. Bluebird. I'm truly sorry for your father's bad turn. I think I'll need to go and see Mr. Tanner now, if you'll excuse me?" It's a question that she doesn't wait to have answered; merely rising and walking away from the younger man and going over to the overall manager's office.

She taps and Tanner's muffled voice comes through the door. Opening it, she wonders if she'll ever dare allow this pent up fury to show. Whole planets could be rocked out of their orbits if she did.

"Mrs. Baxter, come in, come in. Pull the door closed, please? Coffee?" Tanner is all jovial and hearty, very bad sign. "Are you feeling all right, Mrs. Baxter?"

"Frankly, no, Mr. Tanner, I am not feeling the least bit all right."

Tanner doesn't quite know how to respond to this but gestures for her to have a seat on the other side of his desk with the rain sheeting down the window behind him.

"First, we all want you to know that no one blames you for Mr. Bluebird's stroke."

"How reassuring."

"Uh — well, that's important, you know. I imagine his son told you that the doctors were pretty sure he was heading for another stroke no matter what — right?"

"He told me."

"Are you sure you won't have some coffee?"

"I'm sure."

"Well, uh — see, irregardless of Mr. Bluebird's current condition, well, your conduct last night in the dining room was, shall we say, most unprofessional."

"Mr. Tanner?"

"Yes, Mrs. Baxter?"

"Aren't you just flat out tired of how those drunken rednecks keep running over the Gulfview's lawn knocking that lovely wrought iron fence down again and again?"

"What?"

"And how about those lazy micks, sitting around out by the Rite-Aid, leering at the girls from Francis Xavier?"

"Mrs. *Baxter*!"

"I don't know about you," and here Marjean leans in towards the shocked manager and drops her voice, "but I am just sick of Yankees and honkeys coming in here and taking honest black folk's jobs away. Do you know how many honkey-assed northerners we've had as overall manager when there are highly qualified people, people such as myself, who have been passed over?"

"*Mrs.* Baxter, I believe that will be *enough*!"

"It's a bitch, isn't it?"

"What!"

"It is one real bitch to have to sit still and listen to that kind of poisonous garbage and worse without being able to say one single word, isn't it?" She gestures towards the closed door. "That man should *never* have been permitted to use that kind of language here." Now she rises and walks back to the door, looking down her nose at the open-mouthed manager.

"My attorney will be in touch."

She's shaking as she walks out, so she walks real slow with her head, her poor, pounding head, held high. Arnaud is holding out an envelope, probably her last paycheck. He looks like he thinks she'll bite but it's taking all her effort to stay controlled and on top, so she can't smile to reassure him. She takes the envelope and turns to get her coat and umbrella when Missus Myers walks over and hands her a folded piece of paper. She opens it; it's a telephone number.

"I'll call next week and we can get together for lunch, Amanda."

"Wonderful, Marjean. I'm looking forward to it."

Out in the car, with hands trembling so hard she barely open it, Marjean tears at the envelope. Inside is a letter from some law firm. The firm that is representing Mr. Augustin Linders in a lawsuit against the Gulfview Plaza and Mr. Angelo Bluebird. In the middle of tight lines of type is a figure, five figures. Five big figures. She scans the letter on its heavy parchment paper. The big shots up in Atlanta want to settle. She was right, she can sue the velvet off the wallpaper in that hole.

She sits listening to the rain and doesn't start the car right away. The fury is spent and she feels better. Not much, but some better. She even hopes that old Bluebird isn't in pain, poor, old fool. Running her tongue around the inside of her mouth, she's pretty sure she's spat out the last stones.

"You won't need that." Lucy bossed.

Kim knew he wouldn't need a second sweater; they were only going for two nights but that tone just worked on him. He'd once found it endearing.

"I might." Risking a glance over at his wife, Kim continued folding the sweater. "I can't know now which one I'll want to wear."

"You're such a girl." Even as they left her mouth, it looked like Lucy was trying to reel the words back in. Glaring, she left the bedroom, yelling for the kids to hurry up.

Every trip up to the house Kim's folks had left him was a full-scale production and, not for the first time, he thought about putting it on the market. Lucy would never go for that; it meant something to her to have a 'place in the country'.

"Da-a-addy!" Julie was whining, coming up the stairs, "Do we have to go this weekend? I made plans!"

"You want to tell your mother that?" Kim nodded towards the staccato barking coming up from the utility room at the back of the house.

"No! I want you to tell her!" Julie flounced onto the bed, kicking out her bare feet. "You're the parent, too!"

Julie was twelve and the next six years looked to be trying. Kim didn't remember anything in the past dozen years that could have prepared him for raising a teen-age girl. How had that spunky darling thing morphed so quickly into this? It was unfortunate that she sounded so much like Lucy.

"You know we'll have a great time." Kim tried for soothing. If he could calm her down without getting Lucy back up here...

"Nu-uh. I don't know that! There is nothing to *do* up there."

"Then you'll just have to learn how to use your imagination and quit sitting around waiting to be entertained, won't you?" Lucy startled them both mostly with that even, reasonable tone.

Julie wisely held her tongue and slunk out of the room.

"Get your shoes on. Your bag had better be packed because we're leaving in five minutes." Lucy called out over her shoulder before swinging her attention back to Kim. "You ready, yet?"

"Almost."

"It's no wonder the girls never get anywhere on time with you as an example." Lucy's tone was still suspiciously calm and Kim tried to read between the lines.

His final surgery was scheduled for next week and he was still waiting for Lucy to break. Lucy had always been the wild child, teasing Kim on their first date about voting for Reagan. She was the one who wanted to home school the kids, who volunteered at the local food co-op. It had taken a lot to talk her out of naming the girls Luna and Eclipse.

She was the only woman that Kim could be honest with about his special things. When she bought him a red and black garter belt for their first Valentine's Day he proposed. No one got it about Lucy, that her loudness and impatience were her defense. Kim protected her with his name, his success as a respected professional in the sleazy world of high budget advertising and this enormous pre-war apartment overlooking the Hudson, another legacy from parents who never had known what to make of their only son.

"Just this once let's leave the girlie stuff home, ok?" She lowered her voice even though both girls knew that their Daddy was going to be a lady after next week.

"Why?" Kim didn't even own men's underwear.

"Dammit, Kim, haven't you had your way enough yet? Do you really need to do this?"

"This?" Kim had known it was coming and somewhere deep in his belly everything got calm. Let her say it. Let Lucy shoot her most direct shot and be done with it.

Lucy stood there and Kim stood there and the girls stopped whatever they were doing. Julie crept up to the doorway and waited.

No one said anything for days, weeks, eons. Then Julie stepped into the room.

"Leave her alone, Mom. And hurry up; we're going to be late getting out of here and traffic will be murder."

Fallen Apple

On the last Tuesday of October in 1962, a jewel of a day with the kind of blue sky that makes you want to cry, my mother put her notebooks in order, chronologically, and sent a final draft of her last poetry collection to her agent. My sister and I were at our babysitter's so the only one to hear the report of the pistol was our old dog, Grunt. Being the daughter of a famous suicide is a valid career path. One bullet and no door has ever been closed to me.

Can I write?

I can, but it doesn't matter all that much. A powerhouse agency swooped in and poached me away from Mother's perplexed agent, Uncle Bobby, roughly an hour after my second novel was optioned. Uncle Bobby knew when he was beaten and, besides, Mother had taken care of him in her meticulous will. He wished me well and retired to Costa Rica.

My sister went for the cliché of drugs and alcohol.

Her messy memoir is not selling. The market is saturated, true, but it's just badly written. She's still pissed that I declined to add a blurb to the jacket. I hope she's getting to those meetings as I'd prefer she not drink herself to death but I also prefer not to be associated with crap.

I've got this book tour coming up. My second ex, the lazy s.o.b., won alimony in the divorce and I'm writing checks while my assistant packs. I know I can make the payments electronically but it soothes something brutal and sharp inside me to know he has to take the time to go deposit the checks and always has to worry whether his mail will be stolen. Asshole.

Pissed off at me or not, my sister always cashes the monthly check I send. Mother may have hated her fame but she was happy enough to spread the money around and it's been up to me to bring money back to the fame. I snap the checkbook shut and reach for my glass of chilled green tea.

"Excuse me, Miss Seagal, which laptop do you want to take?"

"What? Oh, I don't know, the smallest one, the lightest." Gianna is thorough but annoying and I'd appreciate more initiative on her part.

I pick up the itinerary again; Christ, why does that bastard Dilkin insist on a dartboard approach to booking? Chicago, Atlanta, Portland (Maine), Kansas City (Kansas), Santa Fe, Miami, Boise (Boise?), Dallas, Minneapolis, Portland (Oregon), San Diego, Pittsburgh, Los Angeles and then, finally, New York. When did book tours become a form of punishment? I used to love being the rockstar, didn't I?

"Excuse me, Miss Seagal, should I pack your fur?"

"What do *you* think, Gianna? It's fucking September. Use your brain for something besides separating your ears." She forgets that she's standing behind me facing the mirror and I get the full blast of her silent fury for the second it takes for her to compose herself. I thought this one would work out, but I'm having my doubts. Nothing for it now. It's too late to break in a new one.

And the telephone rings. It's Dilkin. Let him talk to voice mail. Jesus, but he loves the sound of his own voice so no harm, no foul. I motion for Gianna to hand me my hairbrush, aiming my flashiest smile into the mirror. She smiles back and hands it to me. I know I shouldn't but cannot resist one last tiny poke.

"Thanks, G. Call Anton, you need a trim and a threading before we go." I touch my forefinger to the point between my own nicely separated eyebrows and wink.

The phone rings again. Jesus. I don't even look at it, just hand it to Gianna. She's not smiling now. I go back to brushing my hair, not really paying attention until the phone is suddenly thrust at me. Gianna's face is tight.

"It's Mr. Dilkin. Won't take no for an answer."

"Now what?" If nothing else, I can take someone else's head off this morning. Dilkin's grows back pretty quickly.

"Mindy's disappeared. She left a letter."

"What do you mean 'disappeared'? She's always off with some new man. She'll be around to cash her check."

"No, you need to read this letter. She's about to pull some stunt."

"Read it to me."

"Nope, not me. I'm bringing it over." *Click*. Drama queen. And just to heighten the soap opera, he texts: *We may have to ditch tour*.

That suits me, but my publisher isn't going to ditch this tour. Dilkin's gone off his meds or he's been reading my mother's poetry again. Can I add the caveat to my next contract for a publicist that they must have never heard of my mother? It's not so unlikely. After all, it's not as if she was Sylvia fucking Plath for Christ's sake.

"Hide the vodka and put out something to eat. Dilkin's on his way over."

I have read Mindy's letter three times and it's crazier with each reading. But she's not crazy and I need to come up with a plan. Fast. I'm due in Chicago tomorrow evening. Clearly, I've been underestimating my drug-addled little sister for some time now.

This really verges on genius.

"Ok, here's what we're going to do." Gianna and Dilkin actually lean forward. This is the best I have to bring to this little war? I may be in real trouble here. "G., you leave right now and prepare the staff in Chicago. Don't tell them too much, just make sure they know what may happen and what to ignore." She sits there, all expectant and confused. "Go! Now! Go on, you know who to call at the airlines. I want you in Chicago in three hours. Get them ready."

She hustles out and I turn to Dilkin. "You get to Atlanta and do the same. Get going. You know how to handle this."

"We can't leapfrog through the whole tour like this. She'll have already talked to the people in Sante Fe and Boise before we even hit Chicago."

"No, she won't." I know who I have to call now. "She's got to be sure we're playing our part in this before she can approach each next location." I pause, then grab a piece of paper and pen. "Here, get this press release out."

They're gone and now I look at my phone like it's rotted. I have to dial the number because I dumped it from the phone's memory years ago. I doubt I'll ever dump it from my memory, dammit. Two rings, what am I going to say if it goes to voice mail? Oh, let it go to voice mail. I'll think of something.

"That took longer than I thought it would." His voice still does that thing to me.

"Go ahead. Gloat. It gets better: I need your help." I wait.

"Why would I help you?"

"Old time's sake?"

"Not good enough." He's smiling. I can hear it.

"Because your ex-wife is about to wreck my life and my career."

"You'll recall why she's my ex, yes?"

"Don't even. This is a conversation you do not want to start."

"Sure I do. It'll relieve the boredom."

"You're the one who checked yourself into that place, don't whine now if it's not to your liking." I need to watch it, I really do need Ty's help, but Jesus, he gets under my skin.

"This is fun. What kind of mess has my little Mindy unleashed this time?"

"She sent a letter to my publicist and says she's going to commit suicide at one of my readings on this book tour."

"You can't believe she's serious. The woman is so much of a wreck that she still hasn't signed off on the divorce." He goes quiet and I wait. "Since when have you gotten so easily spooked?"

"You didn't read the letter."

"Bring it to me." It's not a request.

"I don't have time. I have to be in Chicago tomorrow. Look, just call her. Talk to her."

"Oh, you are delusional, Cupcake. I can't think of a surer way to have her dangling in front of the Barnes & Noble at State and Elm."

"You're wrong. I seduced you, remember?" Call *me* Cupcake?

"I'll need to read the letter if I'm going to be of any use in this farce."

"I'll courier a copy." No way is this thing going to be accessible online anywhere.

I can feel it happening; those old sticky tendrils of hope. "Thanks." *Click*. Quick.

Am I safe? No, and I never have been around this man. Not from the moment Mindy brought him to my first book release. I shake my head, like I can dislodge something stuck, and arrange a copy of this time bomb delivered to the man who may very well turn out to be the fuse.

I was so impressed with everything back then, including myself. Especially myself.

That book release was like Christmas morning, the first warm day of spring and falling in love all at the same time. The night before, I couldn't close my eyes and was still riding my adrenaline high through the day and into the next night. I wore my first ever couture outfit and when I walked into that room, I owned it.

The fact that half the luminaries in the room were there looking for a fault line, a soft place to pry open and poke around in, only increased my sense of power. They were looking for signs of suicide and I gave them a collective bitch slap. The novel has been proclaimed dead for decades, so it always surprises everyone when another novel takes off. And mine was rocketing out of the stratosphere.

Moving with ease from circle to circle, I made my rounds of the room, sipping one glass of prosecco. Of course I'd had to invite Mindy but had decided that any boneheaded crap she might pull could not touch me. If the vultures wanted a good look at their future suicide Mindy would certainly provide it.

So, when she arrived, I was ready to welcome her with genuine ease. I heard her before I saw her, poor kid totally inherited Father's ghastly titter when she was nervous. I was happy to finish with a certain powerful agent, leaving her to wonder if she'd hooked me or not, and turned to greet my sister.

The worst writers call it a lightning bolt, the better ones will toss a grenade in the general direction, but the best writers aim for that perfect throat shot before squeezing off their round. Every hackneyed cliché crackled and fell when the man standing next to Mindy looked at me. Christ, he wasn't even all that, really. Ty isn't tall, he's not really great looking and he's losing his hair. But what he's got he knows how to use and when he looked at me he took me.

Mindy, being mildly toasted, noticed nothing. She was tricked out in some ridiculous stab at bohemian-cool and launched into her steady stream of consciousness the moment I got in earshot. I reminded myself that she couldn't touch me tonight as heads turned, bent and whispered. Even so, I steered the two of them away from the drinks table.

"Nice turnout." Ty inserted.

"Oh, right! Sorry, sorry," and away she went, winding through an overlong introduction that began with where Ty's parents honeymooned and how he was conceived.

I was not then, and am still not, easily duped.

The warning sirens were blasting and I was sort of paying attention to them. He was trouble. I hadn't had enough trouble at that point to understand why the sirens were so loud. Trouble, in my still soft comprehension, was merely another source of material. My compromise was to go off with him for a second glass of wine, let his arm graze mine and then shuck him off for that still circling agent.

He didn't call or email or make one move in my direction. I stood by an open door, waiting for nothing. I got to work on the next book. The first one got optioned for a movie with some real names signing on to push it to its second life. Time did not do what it's supposed to do and, at least once a day, I checked for something that was not there.

If time wasn't going to do it, I had to take drastic action: I got married.

"She was bluffing all along." Dilkin was on his third scotch after the signing in Pittsburgh.

I hold out my glass. Gianna quit back in Boise, so it's been Dilkin and I slogging across the country like some inane snake oil show. The readers, bless their bored, pointless little hearts, have been lining up. The publisher will be happy although my editor's already been on my ass about the next book.

"We're not home free yet, champ. Don't go and fucking jinx us."

"Oh, come on, you knew she was just messing with your head." He drains the glass and makes to reach for the bottle.

"That's enough." I sweep the bottle out of his reach, topping off my own glass. "We still got LA and then New York to get through and, think about this for just a minute, where would she make a bigger splash than by offing herself there?"

"I can't believe you give her that much space in your head. You know what a ditz she is! Give me that bottle. Just one more." He makes a grab for the bottle, but Dilkin never could hold his liquor and I easily keep it out of reach.

"Go to bed and don't even think of whining about a hangover tomorrow. We're up at eight, no matter what. Got that?"

He grumbles and I feel like I'm dealing with a drunken dog — one that's only partially housebroken. He lurches off to bed and leaves me with the booze and my dirty secret.

At each next destination, each next signing, I've been adrenalized to the hilt, ready for my next big career boost. Now that I think of it, though, yeah, if she's gonna do it, she's gonna do it in LA or New York.

My money's on New York.

It's good. This Friday, it's a good one. I've sold three magazine subscriptions and it's not even noon. I like this town. I didn't like it last night when we pulled in but today I see it's a pretty good town. Ok, no, it's not a city or anything, but I haven't had one door slammed in my face yet. Not one dog has been sicced on me. The ladies who don't want to get our magazines, they apologize like they mean it.

One even offered me lemonade. It tasted terrible but that's ok.

How does a nice middle class boy from Defiance, Ohio wind up with this crazy traveling gang of losers and misfits, pushing lousy magazine subscriptions? It's all Reverend Bailey's fault. He might try to deny it but he's the one who had to go and tell my folks about me and Bobby Lewis.

Someday I'm going to live where no one gives a crap about what I do or who I do it with. Until then, I'm keeping my eyes open.

But hooking up with Mr. Skice and his crew got me out of the fire and that's all I needed. Gives me a chance to get my feet back under me. No one on the crew talks to me much and that's fine. I'm not like them. I don't curse and don't go out for beers at the end of the day. I'm careful. I'm....good. Well, not always. Early in the week I'm useless but by Wednesday something shifts and by Fridays I am very good.

Mr. Skice will tell you how good I am. Actually, no, he won't. *He's* good that way.

Now he's thinking he's got me where he wants me. I can tell by the way he's all rude and dismissive now. Well, all I got to say is that he's in for a surprise in the morning.

Sleet is shredding the apple blossoms when the crew's van pulls out. Spring never lives up to its reputation in these Great Lakes towns. What does? It's Thursday. I smile and wave goodbye even though no one in that old van is looking or would care if they were.

Closing the big front door pricks open both security and panic. She's not an early riser and she can't make a decent glass of lemonade to save her life, but for now, this is good.

Good enough, anyway.

Nights weren't such a goddamned horror show anymore now that the TV didn't go off the air at 2 am. As long as the tube was blabbering, the awfulness was muted. Coming to, he shut the fucking thing off and erased the messages on the machine without listening to them; probably just his daughter calling again. That or bill collectors.

It was going to rain all day. He paused by the screen door, cracking open another beer. If he was lucky, that first slug would hit something and he'd feel all right for awhile. This morning the slug hit nothing and he headed for the john to puke it back up. No dry heaves this time, please, not that. His guts still hurt from that last round.

Somebody up there still loved him and, after plopping out the useless beer he seemed to be done. Just to be sure, he waited, kneeling by the toilet with his head down. Yeah, it was over. Heaving himself up and avoiding the mirror, he splashed water on his face. You couldn't drink the water around here anymore thanks to surface mining. He kept his mouth and eyes shut tight.

Transparent and wrung out, he walked back through to the kitchen. There was the better part of a 12 pack and maybe a quarter bottle of vodka left. He could stay in today if he had to, but he'd have to get out later tonight before Don's closed. Maybe he should just go now. Driving lit up was one thing, but what with the rain and all, it seemed smart to get it done now. Feeling around in his pockets, he found eighteen dollars and some change. Wasn't it still early in the month, like the tenth or something?

The jangling of the telephone just about wrecked him all over again. Damned stupid thing. The answering machine kicked on and there was Penny's voice, just about the last thing he still had of her, sweetly telling whoever not to bother knocking if this trailer was a'rocking.

"Mr. Peterson, it's very important that you contact us right away. We do not want to take legal action, but your last check bounced and your balance with us now stands at well over six hundred dollars. My name is Katie Hammon and my extension is 89."

Crap. Now he would have to get down to Don's for kerosene because it didn't sound like he'd be getting any heating oil for awhile. He ought to get to it right away, too, before the shaking and then the cure for the shaking finished the day for him. Where the fuck were his keys? Toby was scratching at the back door, whining to get in out of the rain. Penny never let Toby in when he was wet. Passing the door, he popped it open and went on into the kitchen to look for his keys. Happy now, the wet dog gave himself a good shake and jumped up into Penny's old chair.

Pinging around the house like a slow-motion pinball, he just could not find those keys. When was the last time he went out? Yesterday, right? Right, cuz he'd driven into town for lottery tickets, that case of beer and the bottle of vodka. He was running his hand up along the top of the fridge when he heard gravel crunching out back. Christ almighty; who the hell?

Toby was on the job, barking at the back door. Wincing at the racket, he pushed the door open and let the dog do his work. Maybe whoever it was would just leave. Toby quit his carrying on. Great. Someone he knew.

"Where the hell you at, you old bastard?"

He'd repaid that twenty so what did Henry want?

"There you are." Henry carried his weight easily, carelessly heaving up the steps onto the back porch. Nodding, he came in from the rain. "You need to get out more, son."

"Nice to see ya, Henry."

"You look like hell."

"Want a beer?"

"No. You got any coffee?" Henry, being Henry, went straight for the bottled water under the table, "You gonna wash these dishes or you just want to save time and pitch 'em?"

The place was a sorry mess, but he wasn't in the mood. Instead, he went and got that beer for himself.

"You got another smoke?"

Henry shook one out of the pack. This beer may not be tripping any hidden switches, but it did taste ok.

"When's the last time you et?"

"Quit it."

"So, what, you just gonna drink your sorry ass to death?"

"Quit. It." He lit the cigarette and looked out at the rain.

"You know damn well I ain't gonna," Henry accepted a light, nodding, "I got a job for you."

"You can't afford me." The rain was letting up some, maybe this would be a good time to get on down to Don's and get rid of Henry. "And besides, I'm retired." Where the *fuck* were those keys?

"You aren't retired, chief; you are unemployable."

"Well, there you go then," He stood up, "Look I got things to do. Nice seeing you."

"A liar as well as a drunk. Damn son, your soul is the devil's for sure," Henry stayed put. Toby was back at the door, now he wanted out, "I know you need the cash."

A thought occurred and, sure enough, the keys were under his bed. How the hell?

"Look, I got to go," He called from the bedroom.

"Peterson, you damned fool," Henry was standing in the doorway with two cups of coffee, "Drink this, take a shower for God's sake and come on down to Miss Amy's with me." He set one cup on the dresser.

Miss Amy. She couldn't still be alive, could she? The coffee was bitter, over-brewed. Too hot. Absently, he blew on it and sipped. What the hell was that old stick doing now? Miss Amy never stocked beer or any kind of liquor in that little store of hers, so he hadn't been there in some twenty years. What kind of cash? What kind of work? How long since he'd showered? Whew!

Stepping into the tub, he was careful. He'd begun to shake a little. That coffee hadn't been a great idea. He steadied himself and reached for the soap. Penny'd been right about how they ought to have considered replacing the old hot water heater. Bitch.

He couldn't remember why he hadn't showered in so long, the hot water felt that good. It felt like layers of rot were coming off him. He almost expected to be a different color or something when he grabbed the one mostly clean towel.

Nope, he was the same color and everything. Nothing had changed except that he was really starting to shake now.

"Bring me a beer, would ya?" He called out to Henry. Maybe he could pick a fight and get the fat bastard out of here. Maybe he could chance the vodka. He pulled some clothes on. Laundry. He really did need to wash some clothes although this shirt wasn't so bad.

"Here ya go, chief. We can take my truck." Henry handed him a cold beer. Son of a bitch.

"Whatever."

The beer helped. He didn't slam any part of himself into the door of Henry's Chevy. The rain was steady as misery, but warmer. Maybe he could put off the kerosene until tomorrow or something. Henry put the old Chevy in gear, flipped on the radio and eased down the drive and out to the blacktop.

"How the hell old is Miss Amy anyway?" He drained the beer and set the empty between his feet, "Hard to believe she's still vertical."

"She ain't," Henry held out his hand for that empty, "Miss Amy's been dead for over five years, some towelhead bought her place. Has his whole damned family running the store." He reached out the window and neatly flipped the empty beer can into the bed of the truck.

The rain gained weight. What the hell kind of work was Henry talking about anyway? In a kinder world, the rain would have let up some as they pulled into Miss Amy's old place. Instead it was like someone turned a faucet on full force and there was nothing for it but to run. Inside, he was off balance. The pitted wooden counter was gone. The floor was clean tile. And the light, Christ, in this light Henry looked like an extra in a zombie movie.

A reedy, too friendly voice greeted them, offering coffee and asking about the ride over.

"Thanks, Ahmed, that'd be great. This here's my friend I was telling you about, the consultant."

Consultant? He shuffled around to the stack of newspapers, glancing up to nod. Not really paying attention, he began to go through the stack, scanning front pages. Henry and his new best friend were murmuring over by the counter. He picked up the only local paper still around, The Eagle, and then about dropped it, not believing his eyes.

There he was on the front page. That was him all right, back behind the table of town council members, wearing a suit and tie, but still looking like a gut shot dog. He stared, then flipped the paper over to see if some answer was below the fold. This was yesterday's paper and the date of the council meeting was last Wednesday. Peering closer, he couldn't deny that that was really him, right down to the dent in his chin that he got from his Daddy.

"You ok, chief?" Henry touched his arm and about sent him through the roof.

Penny used to tell him he was a blackout drinker and that, if he didn't get help, she was leaving. Then she left.

"Yeah, well. So what's this job?" The old noggin wasn't completely shot.

"Easy, chief, come on over here and act civilized," Henry eased them back to the counter.

The newspaper felt hot and he stifled the need to look again, taking the coffee instead. He couldn't believe he was having more coffee; Christ, he was going to be clawing at the walls soon if he didn't get some vodka. Finally Henry got to the damned point.

"Let's take a look at that floor, ok?"

Almost immediately a small, shrouded figure appeared at the cash register and Ahmed led the two men to the far corner of the store where, sure enough, the floor sloped visibly down into the corner.

"You're in luck here, Ahmed, my friend is not just a master carpenter, but he's a damned fine engineer as well. He is the man for the job."

"Can't really get any idea as to what's what with this rain," He ran a shaking hand through his hair. Jesus, some vodka please? "I'll have to come back when the rain's done."

Before things got worse, he spun around and went over to the shelf with the diluted booze and picked up two fifths. He wasn't proud and let Henry pay for his booze. The need was on and he had less than twenty bucks to get through the month.

· · · ·

It was the middle of the night when he came to and put the lights on to look at that newspaper again. Dumbfounded, he went to the fridge and got a beer. Back on the couch, he peered more closely at that photo. No one seemed to notice the criminal in the background. Gritting his teeth, he finally just read the damned article.

Sinkholes. The mining company was dodging responsibility for two new sinkholes, one of which had apparently eaten the First Methodist Church. How had he missed that? Ok, so he hadn't been to church since someone's funeral, but Jesus. And then it hit him, what was wrong with that sloping floor in Ahmed's place.

Rising, pacing, he tried to slow his head down. He paused at the door, listening to the rain. No let up. Good Christ, couldn't he ever catch even one lousy break? Pulling on his slicker, he whistled for Toby and went out to the truck. Once in the truck, he stopped and tried to think. Henry. He'd need that fat bastard for sure tonight. Back into the house. He lit a cigarette and dialed Henry's number. Eight rings, fourteen rings, lost count.

"This'd better be good, goddamnit."

"Yer buddy's store is about to go down into a sinkhole. I'll meet you there in ten."

"What the hell are you talking about?"

"You can call the county, too, if you want. But we got to get that towel head and his family outta there now," He hung up, time was squishing in on itself and it might be too late already.

He couldn't remember rain like this ever. Black, slippery and by the bucket. Toby was whining and he wondered if this was it; if he was about to skid off the side of the hill, but nope. The wheel stayed steady.

Wait a minute. He was already at the edge of town. What the? He slowed, pulled over and then eased back out onto the road. Now he was paying attention, watching for it and he still missed the drive to Miss Amy's old store. This was nuts. Gauging that he had to be in the general area, he pulled the hood of his slicker up and got out. He held the door for Toby who just sat there, whining. This was the kind of best friend he always seemed to attract. Fuck you, Penny.

Here it was. The drive was right here, clear as day. The wind turned and he had to drop his head, shouldering into the storm like it was a stalled car needing to be pushed. The drive widened and he was in the parking lot, water streaming over the gravel. Squinting, he raised his head just as a set of headlights swept the scene.

No store. No store? But wait, way over there. What was that? Henry pulled up next to him, left the headlights on and got out. Together, they fought the wind and got over to where Ahmed huddled with his family. As they got closer, the small woman's screams rose above the storm.

Ahmed was holding her or she'd be in the pit. Henry went over and formed another barrier. No one else wanted anywhere near that hole, but he had to see. Like a broken doll house, the top of the store was angled bad and three sides were caved in. He strained, was that a baby's wail? No, it was the wind. Something bumped his leg and he about jumped into the hole before seeing that it was Toby.

The sirens came. The authorities came and the ladies' auxiliary came and Ahmed and his tattered family were bundled off to the hospital. Henry pulled him away from the hole.

"Yer coming home with me, chief," Henry's grip was inescapable, "C'mon, Toby, get in."

Once inside the cab, Henry tossed him a towel and he wiped his face.

"They couldn't get to the baby in time. The older kids ran, but it went down too fast and the baby's ... down there."

He didn't say anything. Lighting a smoke from Henry, he just stared out at the road ahead of them.

"This'll put a fire under some asses."

Henry always did talk too much. They pulled into Henry's place and he got out, whistled for Toby and set out down the road. No way was he spending the night listening to this crap.

"You stupid bastard, where the hell you going?"

Now, of course, the rain was easing up and it wasn't that long a walk up the holler to home. He went back to trying to get his head around that photo in the paper. When was that council meeting? What was he doing last Wednesday anyway? Sitting in front of the tube, drinking. What else? Something else was swimming up. His daughter had called. Something about .... Wait. Penny? Hospital? It wasn't coming back, but it was bad whatever it was.

Rounding the last turn and coming out by the red bud she'd planted when they first got this place, he was relieved to see the trailer still sitting there. Superstitiously, he stamped his feet hard as he could. Ahmed probably thought the ground was solid under his place, too. There was no telling.

Indoors, he shucked himself out of his wet things and went for a beer. Absently, he popped it open and took that first blessed pull. Now this was just weird. He looked at the can like it would tell him what was going on and then took another pull. He'd never drank because he liked the taste of the stuff, but now there was nothing, no taste at all. Worse, there was no hit.

Frowning, he went back into the kitchen. Up in the cupboard was some full-strength vodka from the state store and that would tell the story. He hadn't bothered with a glass for years and just took a good, healthy slug right from the bottle. Now this was just annoying; nothing. No burn, no nothing.

He waited for the panic, then tossed the bottle into the trash. Jesus, this place was a stinking mess. As daylight took over, he found himself clearing up piles of dirty clothes and dishes. He lit a smoke and put the radio on. When the phone rang, it was like he was expecting the call and answered it.

"Hey, hon." It was his daughter.

"No, baby, I'm fine but what's going on with Penny?" He sat down and listened, stroking Toby's ears. "I can drive up later today; we had another sink hole last night so I didn't get any sleep yet."

Idly, he reached over and picked up that damned newspaper. For some reason, he thought he wouldn't be in the photo now, but there he was and nothing in that picture had changed. He finished up the call with Christie and went back to work.

About the Author

T. Remington is a Pushcart Finalist who has been writing and publishing short fiction and essays for over twenty five years. She lives in Harlem with her partner in life and art, AleXander Hirka. Basically she writes because she can't not write.